INSIDE THE NIGHT

Inside the Night
Copyright © 2021 Madeline Dyer
All rights reserved.

This story was first published by Five Points Press in *Unbound: Stories of Transformation, Love, and Monsters* in 2021.

This edition published in January 2024 by Ineja Press

Cover Design by Sarah Anderson
Interior Formatting by Sarah Anderson

Paperback ISBN: 978-1-912369-38-6
eBook ISBN: 978-1-912369-37-9

The author can be contacted via email at
Madeline@MadelineDyer.co.uk

Second edition, January 2024

INSIDE THE NIGHT

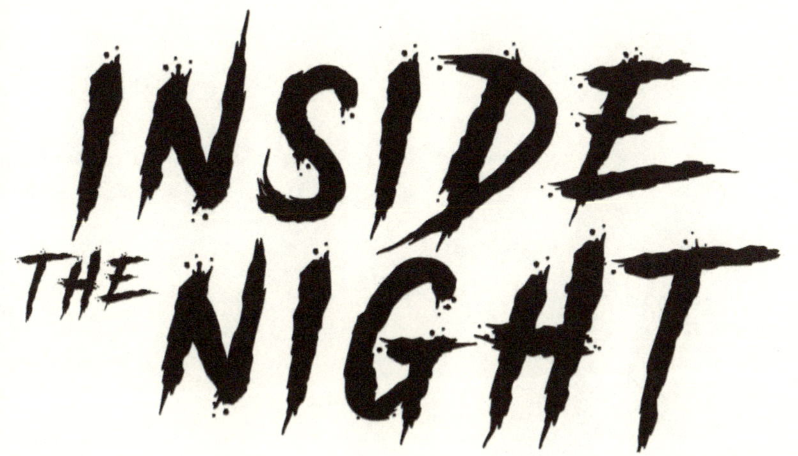

MADELINE DYER

INEJA PRESS

For all the Medusas out there

Local Schoolgirl Found Dead in Suicide

BLACKTHORNE—The body of eighteen-year-old Maliah Swan was found in Blackthorne Woods in the early hours of yesterday morning, below the west tower of Blackthorne Castle. Mr. Reynolds, head-teacher at Blackthorne Community College—England's highest-achieving school for those aged 11-18 years—said Maliah was a promising student who had her sights set on Oxford University. Her loss will be sorely felt by all who knew her.

ONE

In the darkest corner of the darkest town, a small boy stands with his hands raised up to the sky. Allie watches him from her window, her cigarette smoldering in her fingers. She knows she shouldn't be able to see him, not when it's so dark, but the Power has done strange things to her eyes. She only has to hone in on something—*someone*—in the darkness, and her vision gets brighter, sharper, clearer. Allie almost wishes it wouldn't. It would be easier not to watch the transformations taking place. But she is transfixed, as always.

Allie takes a puff of her cigarette. The smoke hits the back of her throat, gritty, raw. She's still not used to it. But Riko suggested it would help calm her anxiety.

INSIDE THE NIGHT

No one should do anything that Riko says, especially not Allie. He's an O'Donovan. She doesn't even know how she can look at Riko so calmly each day and not want to kill him. But she does look at him calmly, and she takes his advice. Three days ago, she took the cigarette pack he offered her, too.

Allie mused over that gift for a long time, and she still thinks about it now, as she tries to work out whether the cigarettes are a peace offering. Or maybe even a message that says 'I believe you.' Riko might feel guilty about what Kyle did to her, about how the whole town treated her. And if he does, maybe that means not all the O'Donovans are bad.

Or maybe she's thinking too deeply about all of this. What Kyle did happened four months ago, after all, and with everything that's now happening with the stonifications, she's sure Riko's not giving it any thought. At any rate, she supposes he's right: smoking does calm her anxiety. Because she's not shaking with fear and constantly thinking about Ellie as she watches the small boy in the street. Sweat isn't running down her spine in torrents, sticking her shirt to her back. She's just . . . there. Watching it all, a picture of calmness. Even though she's not really feeling it. What's happening can't sink into her now, because the cigarettes have provided a barrier. A numbness. Or maybe it's the alcohol that did that. She's not really sure.

When her mind is numb, she can't think about that night, the night it all started. And when she doesn't think about that night, it's like it never actually happened. Like Kyle never held her down on the scratchy carpet that smelt of cat piss while he mocked her, called her *baby*. The haze of the nicotine and alcohol rewrites the past, and Allie likes that. She should be in charge of her own story.

The boy's trying to move his arms—she can see the concentration on his face. He's not a screamer, and she's glad. Those are always the worst to watch. By now, he's probably too far gone. He'll no longer know his name, no longer know where he is. All he'll know is that he must lift his hands to the sky. Because that's what all of them do, the Night Worshippers. His fingers are offerings to whatever being is up there, the Power that is getting stronger and stronger. The Power that appeared eighteen nights ago.

Sometimes, Allie thinks she must be immune, that she won't ever succumb to the Power—not the way the majority of the town's other residents have. She'll never become a statue—she's convinced of it, at times. Because the Power's given her night vision instead. And it wouldn't do that if it was just going to claim her anyway, would it?

But no one knows.

Allie, her best friend Aion, Riko, and the others in their team appear to be the only survivors in Blackthorne. There aren't many people left alive in England now—most fled after the second night and most who stayed became Worshippers. Of the survivors—or the stupid remainers, depending on who you ask—Allie is the only one with a power. Not that she's told anyone.

So maybe others have the powers too. The best-kept secrets, because everyone's looking for someone to blame. The witch-hunts started after the third night—roving gangs of men and women who kill anyone they think could be behind the stonifications. There are still angry mobs out there, even if many of the hunters have been stonified.

The witch-hunts may not be happening near her town anymore—the last reports she heard were that the hunters were going north—but she's not stupid. Tell someone she has a gift? She'd be the next poor sod hunted down—and she wouldn't put it past Riko not to kill her himself. He's an O'Donovan, even if he does seem a bit nicer than Kyle and the others. He—or whichever hunter came after her—would think she deserved it, that somehow, this was all stemming from her, just because she's got a power and everyone calls the thing in the sky *the Power.*

People invariably see patterns and connections where there aren't any.

That's what Riko's always saying, anyhow. He's the leader of Allie's team.

Only a few days in or so, after it became obvious that the Power that had taken over the night wasn't going away, the teams started to spring up across the country. The police and the army and the scientists weren't doing a great deal. The government were running daily conferences and live press announcements of their proposed actions—until the prime minister himself turned to stone on camera, with the whole country watching. Allie laughed darkly when that happened—it was the PM's own fault for doing the live update at night. He should've known better.

The stonification's only happening in England and Wales—so far. Twitter's full of Americans laughing about it. Only last week, a group of New Zealand teenagers made a video where they pretended to have caught the 'stone disease' too. They just wanted to go viral as the first case of stonification outside of the UK—but it was clear by their laughter that they didn't really believe it. Allie doesn't understand why other countries aren't helping them.

In Blackthorne, Riko was the one to gather up all the survivors. When he found Allie, he went white. Very white. Like he'd seen a ghost.

"What?" Allie said defensively. She wasn't pleased to see him—an O'Donovan. Sure, he'd not been directly involved in the bullying, in trying to discredit her worth to the whole town, but he was still part of that family.

"I thought you were dead?" He swiped at his head before shaking it hard. "I'm sure you were. You . . ." His face paled. "No . . . that's not . . . that can't be right," he said, his eyes on her. "Is the Power affecting anyone else's memory?"

Allie didn't know what he was talking about—and everyone else looked at him like he'd lost his mind. A moment later, he dropped the subject, and didn't bring it up again—but his eyes lingered on her for the rest of the night, heavy with suspicion and lit with a hint of fear. Sometimes she catches him looking at her that way still.

It makes her furious. By rights, Allie should be suspicious of *him*.

She finishes her cigarette, trying not to think of what her parents would say if they saw her drinking and smoking, as she watches the boy's final moments. As always, his hands are the last to turn to stone. The boy's fingers twitch twice, then no more.

The night air is cold through her open window. It is still outside. Silent. Until she hears voices.

Three men in their twenties, all drunk and loud, are staggering toward the boy. They see him, thanks to the flashlights on their phones, and they're laughing and shouting in a foreign language, until their flashlights flicker out.

Tourists, Allie thinks, darkly. Blackthorne still gets a lot of them now. Before, holidaymakers would come to see Blackthorne Castle—the oldest semi-ruined castle in Devon, infused with mythology and stories. But now everywhere in Blackthorne is a destination because people want to see the town where the stonifications started. Tour companies charge boatfuls of curious tourists extortionate amounts to cross the English Channel to see the "Land of the Petrified."

There are so many national and international visitors to Devon and elsewhere now, all wanting to visit the stone people. Tourists aren't affected, so long as they leave by nightfall. At night, anyone in the area is fair game.

A lot of the tour companies even supply their clients with booze; it's no wonder half of the tourists never leave, not when they're too inebriated to remember that they need to leave before night falls. Or maybe some are just cocky and think it won't affect them. That because they're not from England they'll be safe—but they never are. It doesn't matter where you're from, it just matters where you are when night arrives. Allie can't imagine what sort of person would set up tours and sell people tickets to see this, knowing their clients will be in danger if they don't get back to the boat in time.

And Allie's town isn't anywhere near the sea.

"Damn it," one of the men mutters, shaking his phone. But the phone is dead.

All their phones are dead now. It's what happens at night. Cell phones die—sooner, if you're outside. The indoor ones will splutter out by midnight too. Come the next morning, they're all fine, though, because that's when the Power's sleeping.

Silence falls.

And they know what's coming. Everyone knows.

Allie's kidneys hurt a little more than usual as she watches them. She didn't think she'd enjoy watching this—but she does, in a dark, weird kind of way. Something that she'd never admit. She knows men like these—the type who think they own everything, who think they're entitled to girls, who think they're the bee's knees.

Allie wouldn't say she's a violent person; she's only wished death upon three people, and one of them she didn't even really mean it. But she finds she likes watching these men as they run from the darkest corner of the darkest town, because she knows what's coming.

And so do they.

It's almost funny, that they think they can escape it.

Because no one can.

No one outruns the curse once they've offered themselves to the night.

TWO

"All across England we have reports of more of these *stonification* incidents," the reporter on the 10 o'clock news says. He's a good-looking man, but he looks scared now. Worried. He's speaking from France though. He'll be safe there. The Power's only in England. For now—because Allie is sure that one day, it'll spread. She's not sure why she thinks that, she just sort of feels it—and so far, she's been right about how it progressed, starting off only in her town, radiating outward, reaching the nearest city, then swallowing the county, before pockets across the whole of England started succumbing to it.

"The curse has already decimated the epicenter of its origin," the reporter continues.

Decimated the epicenter of its origin. Allie snorts. *She's* still alive, and her town's classed within the epicenter location. And she's not the only one. There are seven others on her team.

If they survive the night. She swallows hard. She doesn't like being alone in the evenings now—wrapped up in duvets, flinching at the slightest creak of a floorboard. The days are okay—because that's when she sees the rest of her team. When Riko allocates them all jobs and when they pretend like they're making progress fighting the Power in the sky.

In the day, Allie can pretend she's stronger than she is. But at night, she only has her cigarettes and booze, pilfered from the now-almost-empty supermarket shelves, and the TV for a distraction until the signal disappears. The welcome, numbing haze isn't enough to stop her feeling scared then. At night, Allie wishes someone in her household was still alive, so she'd have company.

She taps her foot as she watches the rest of the news on her phone. Then her alarm blares. Time for her meds.

After she's taken her Cefalexin and methenamine hippurate, and forced down an apple because the Cefalexin is always easier on her gut if she takes it with food, she checks the websites that log all the incidences of whatever it is that's happening to everyone here. The transformation has got various names: stonification, becoming stoned (that's her favorite), possession by the beast, petrification, succumbing to the curse, becoming a Night Worshipper. No one really knows what to call it.

If you'd told her this would happen a year ago, Allie would have laughed at you and asked what you'd taken. Not now though. Not when she's seen what the Power—as everyone is calling it, after the sky got darker that first night and a sonic boom went off—did to Ellie, her older sister. Graham, Blackthorne's greengrocer, found Ellie after her possession, on the morning of day two. She'd been one of the victims of the first night, along with seven-hundred-odd other residents.

Allie looks toward the cupboard under the stairs, where Ellie now lives. It hadn't been easy getting her in there. The statues are heavy, and most people leave them wherever they are when they get cursed now. It was only after that first night that people desperately tried to bring their loved ones back into their homes.

Allie and her father hadn't spoken about it—moving Ellie wasn't a decision they'd come to together over a cup of coffee. It had been a split-second decision, after Graham had phoned them to say he'd found Ellie, and yes, he was afraid it had happened to her too. *Terribly sorry,* he'd said when Allie and her father had reached Regent Street.

It had been strange, looking at Ellie like that. She didn't look like Allie's sister anymore—not when her eyes were grey. When all of her was grey and solid. Stone. A statue wearing clothes.

Her dad had sworn a lot when they were moving her, and Ellie's arm had banged against the inside of the front door, chipping three of her fingers and causing a crack to spread around her wrist. Allie often wonders what her mother would say if she saw the careless way her daughter had been brought back into the house. Maybe she'd wish that she'd taken Ellie and Allie with her two years ago when she'd fled to France to escape Allie's dad's alcoholism. Instead, she'd only taken Sarah, Allie's oldest sister.

Allie doesn't know why her mom left the two of them behind. She tries to pretend she doesn't think about why her mum hasn't been in contact now, either. The woman's probably eating cheeses and croissants and whatever else the French eat, watching all the drama unfold in Blackthorne and thinking that both Allie and Ellie are dead. Gone. Stoned. That's why her mum hasn't come for her—because she thinks she's too late. That's what Allie tells herself in the small moments where she wonders.

Now, Allie's coat is draped over Ellie's arm. Hides the damage to her wrist. Plus, it's convenient because her sister makes a good coat rack. And her dad isn't here now to tell her to *show more respect*. He's outside. Forever stuck looking up at the gutters. She'd told him not to leave the house. Not when it was starting to get dark. But he'd insisted on day five. Always thought he knew best on everything.

Allie looks at the clock. Sunrise isn't until 7:25 tomorrow. Nine and a half hours to go. She stares around the room, at the peeling paint, sick of the four walls. It should be easy to stay inside at night, knowing what can happen if you don't. But it isn't.

Every night, the Power turns people into Night Worshippers. The first ones it gets are always those who are not in their own homes. Whether they're in the streets or fields or in other people's houses, the Power gets them. It's as if being inside your own house provides some kind of protective ward.

But now the Power must be getting hungrier—or stronger—because it's started summoning people from their homes. The first time this happened, Allie got hysterical—insisting it didn't matter if the other members of their team stuck to their own houses at night, demanding for someone to stay with her—but Aion calmed her down. Told her it made sense for them to return to their own houses at night in case the wards still offered some protection. Allie trusts Aion, and she agreed. So now she stays in her house in the middle of town, and everyone else stays in their houses, and she hopes that the Power's not feeling greedy.

Allie's arms and legs itch and feel fizzy. Too much pent-up energy. She wants to run and run. She used to love running at night, with Aion. The two of them would jog on the moors, practicing for their cross-country competitions.

But that was before Allie got her kidney problems. Now, some days, she can hardly move because of the pain.

And, in any case, nightly runs have stopped now.

Everything's stopped.

People stay inside at night. People try to flee the country in the day, or, if they're remainers like Allie, they gather food from the shops with broken windows. They meet in houses as they try to come up with plans to beat the Power, to save the already stoned, to make life go back the way it was.

Allie misses school. Misses the days when her only worries were getting Mr. Richards's homework done in time, and whether or not Carly and the other popular girls were going to pick on her that day, and whether her father would be drunk when he eventually got home. She even misses all the endless doctors and hospital appointments. Her illness feels even more scary now it's not being monitored.

ALLIE WANTED TO be an artist, before all this started. When she was often bedbound due to pain, she'd doodle in her sketchbooks. She was fascinated with Greek mythology—Medusa, most of all—and she drew her all the time.

A year ago, when she was sixteen, Allie's art class started studying Greek myths too. Allie was delighted. Drawing these figures was what she was good at.

Ms. Symons, the art teacher, assigned each student what she called a 'character'—one of the gods or goddesses, deities, Titans, giants, or mortals. Allie was disappointed to get Penelope rather than Medusa, but nonetheless, she sat next to Aion and tried to stay out of the firing line of Carly and her gang, who loved to throw paint at anyone who wasn't wearing the latest designer clothes.

"Oh, it's hardly made your outfit worse," Carly would say with a snigger, after she'd just pelted a red blob of acrylic at some poor kid's hoodie.

Carly mocked everyone—but for some reason, she hated Allie most of all. She made fun of Allie's father's drinking and her mother's desertion, getting the whole of her gang to join in. It had been humiliating, and even though Allie wasn't violent by nature, in that instant she wanted Carly to die. She didn't want to *kill* her—not like how she'd later want to stab Kyle—just for something bad to happen to her. Like for her to fall down a well. Or go missing.

Just something.

There was only one person that Carly and her gang never touched: Kyle O'Donovan. He was the most popular boy in their year. The best-looking—many of the girls agreed upon that. And he was an O'Donovan—the town's most influential family. Most people in Blackthorne practically worshipped them.

Allie and Aion often sat behind Kyle in art class, as if proximity to him could protect them, like an invisible forcefield. That was, until Carly got wise to their game and had one of her minions summon Kyle to the supply cupboard, under the promise of making out with him. Then Carly flicked black ink all over Aion and Allie, laughing.

Covered in ink, Allie stood up, anger fueling her as she stared across at Carly with her perfect hair and perfect skin—never a pimple in sight—and perfect clothes. A burning desire rose in her to inflict hurt and rage, to make Carly pay.

But *of course* she didn't do anything because Allie was meek then, scared of Carly and the other kids from old money. Instead, she looked down, right at Kyle's artwork. To Allie's disgust, he'd been assigned

Medusa. He'd drawn her severed head in copper tones—and it was this sheen that had caught her attention, as if Medusa herself had called Allie's name. The snakes of her hair almost seemed alive. Little snakes with little thoughts and feelings.

Fury filled her. That wasn't Kyle's original work—that was hers! Allie had drawn that exact portrait last year—the same style, image, and media. The old art teacher had dished out so much praise when she'd turned it in as her homework response to the prompt of 'beauty.' Everyone had seen it, including Kyle—he'd always been in her classes, right from when they were little children at the primary school. He'd even admired her work, saying the snakes were cool—the nicest thing he'd ever said to Allie. Everyone knew he was obsessed with snakes. Even had a pet one.

But now he'd copied her, and Allie was shaking with anger.

Leaving the copying aside, what had Ms. Symons been thinking, giving Medusa to someone like Kyle? The Gorgon should've been assigned to Allie, not him. Or to any of the girls, apart from Carly and her gang.

When Ms. Symons assigned Medusa to Kyle, she'd told the class Medusa was a symbol of female empowerment, but Allie knew the truth: Medusa might be strong, but she was also a victim. She'd been raped by Poseidon and became pregnant with Pegasus and Chrysaor. But was Poseidon punished? Of course not! It was Medusa who was punished. Athena transformed her beautiful hair into snakes and gave her the curse of turning anyone she looked at to stone. And then, if that wasn't bad enough, poor Medusa was beheaded by Perseus, an arrogant and entitled man who'd held onto her head, using it and her petrifying gaze as a weapon.

Kyle wouldn't understand Medusa's trauma. He'd just think her powers were *cool* and *awesome* and keep her silent, an image on his page. If Allie'd had Medusa for this project, she would've found a way to give the woman a voice. To show the world what evil had been done to her. And she certainly wouldn't have copied another student's work.

Allie complained to Aion about Kyle's copying and the teacher's poor job of assigning the figures. She'd told him that Ms. Symons should've assigned Aion the Greek god of eternity, who he was named after, instead of the Moirai—the Fates who control the life thread. And the teacher should've realized that Kyle had copied Allie's work—her painting of Medusa was up in the art block for a whole month last year. Ms. Symons really was stupid. She couldn't see what—or who—was right in front of her eyes.

But Aion didn't seem to care, which annoyed her. Of all people, her best friend—who was named after a god—should've understood.

Allie thinks of that class a lot now, mostly because of Kyle's drawing of Medusa. How he didn't quite manage to copy the finesse of it, how his lines were cruder, more careless, creating a version of Medusa that was close to her own, but not quite. Kyle's drawing haunts her, probably because of Riko.

Kyle was a victim of the first night and in tribute to him, Riko tattooed the snakes from the picture of Medusa onto his own arms, depicting Kyle's copy of Allie's artistry like a bad version of the telephone game. She bets Riko doesn't even know that she was the original artist of that picture, and now he obliviously sports her marks.

When Allie asked him about his tattoos, all Riko talked about was that his brother had been obsessed with Medusa—as if a monster like Kyle O'Donovan cared about a woman preyed upon, victimized, and weaponized! Kyle hadn't been obsessed with the real Medusa, the one that Allie understood and felt connected to. He'd just been preoccupied with snakes because he'd thought they were cool—and because of what they represented: power over others.

That was one of the last things he said to Allie in that room that smelled of cat piss. Some stupid joke about how Allie wasn't powerful at all. How she was just a woman.

Allie's thoughts darken, and she tries to push the memories away. Tries to shove them in a box, somewhere in the depths of her mind, where they can't spill out and taunt her.

She won their war, the one between her and Kyle. Because she's still alive, and not turned to stone. But she can't help but feel like she's forgotten something huge.

Something important.

THREE

"We have to do something," Allie says, glancing at the rest of the team. It is the next morning, finally. She swallows several times, but her throat feels thick, like the pills she took are stuck in it even though she knows they're not.

"We need to find out the cause," Riko says, resting his beefy forearms on Allie's kitchen table. The team always meets at Allie's house because her house is centrally located.

Allie stares at Riko's muscles—elaborate designs of serpents swirl around his upper arms, while lizards with huge, protruding fangs adorn his forearms—and she feels bad because she can't stop. She should be repulsed by him. No matter if he gives her cigarettes and advice, the O'Donovans cannot be trusted. They are bad people. But Riko is Allie's leader because he is the strongest person in their team and for some reason that made the others vote for him. Not that strength stops you becoming stoned.

"The cause is the Power," Aion mutters, rolling his eyes.

Riko ignores him. "We need more information on that sonic boom." He points at Dan, the thirty-one-year-old firefighter. "That's your job for today."

Riko likes bossing people about—even someone ten years or more his senior. That's the problem with the O'Donovans. That, and they're not used to being told no.

He doles out more jobs. Vera and Oliver, the two eldest members of their team—both in their early eighties—are to go to the library and continue looking through the archives. Helen, the sixty-six-year-old music teacher, is to loot more food from the supermarkets. Kiersten and Gabe, a nurse and a physiotherapist, are to try more 'reviving techniques' on the statues.

Riko is still certain that the transformation is reversible. Maybe he just wants to believe that because Kyle, his parents, and his bossy old uncle are no more than decorative pieces on his lawn, around the town, in their beds, now.

He saves the two of them for last. "And Allie and Aion, search through social media."

INSIDE THE NIGHT

It's *always* social media for them. As if they'll magically find that someone has cured the Night Worshippers and decided to tweet the remedy rather than report it on the news.

"What will you be doing?" Aion asks Riko dryly.

"What I always do," he barks back, his hand on the knife in his belt. Allie's noticed he always has that on him now. "Trying to find more survivors."

When he says this, the snakes on Riko's arms seem to hiss. They make Allie shudder.

"HOW ARE YOU doing?" Kiersten pauses on her way out, asking Allie the question she always dreads. "Any more pain?"

Allie shrugs. The pain's about the same.

At least she's still got her meds. It was just luck that the doctor prescribed her new supply before the Power arrived in the sky. Allie has got six weeks of the pills left, and she thinks surely by the time she needs a refill, the world will have righted itself again.

They'll have found a way to reverse the stonifications of all the doctors and nurses and pharmacists. And then she'll definitely get better. Or better than she is now, anyway.

"How's the frequency?" Kiersten asks.

Shame clouds Allie's face, and she looks across at Aion. She knows he's listening, and she hates talking about this with anyone, let alone with him in earshot. He may be her best friend, but some things are just embarrassing.

Allie's kidney problems started as a UTI that just wouldn't go. She'd take the three-to-five days of antibiotics her doctor prescribed, and she'd improve while she was on them. But as soon as she stopped, the UTI symptoms would return. Then the UTI got into her kidneys, and treatment wasn't prompt. Back-to-back dipstick tests showed blood in her urine, and the infection had scarred her kidneys. Her blood tests began to show impaired renal function and doctors talked of the possibility of chronic kidney disease. Her blood pressure got higher, and scans revealed kidney stones. And still she had the UTI symptoms and kidney infection symptoms. It was a constant ebb and flow of them.

Finally, Allie saw a specialist who diagnosed her with an embedded infection that had got under the biofilm of her urinary tract system, scarring her bladder and kidneys. She'd been started on high-dose antibiotics and an antibacterial, and told she'd be on them for nine months at least. Meanwhile, her renal function would be monitored and she was to have regular tests done, counting her numbers of white blood cells and epithelial cells in her urine.

That's definitely not something she wants to talk to Kiersten about in front of Aion and the others who are still making their way out of her house, so Allie just whispers, "it's getting a bit better," even though it's not.

"I WILL SAVE you, Ellie," Allie whispers, looking toward the cupboard under the stairs where her sister is stashed. She and Aion are on the sofa, and she is supposed to be scrolling through Twitter feeds and Facebook pages.

But her mind is on Ellie.

Sorry, she wants to say, because she didn't make sure her sister was back home before dark and the last words she'd said to Ellie weren't kind ones. Ellie had been complaining about how Allie's 'story' was affecting her, how her friends had dropped her too and she'd been given a warning at work. But it wasn't a story—it was the truth.

Allie wants to scream it from the rooftops, make everyone hear her—the voice they tried to silence. Because no one believed her when she spoke up about what Kyle had done. Everyone turned against her.

Kyle's parents shunned her, spread lies about her being unstable and ill. Kyle and Carly made her life hell at school. *Slag* was written on her locker, no matter how many times she and the cleaners scrubbed it off. And her father, who worked for Kyle's uncle, nearly lost his job, because the O'Donovans are—were?—so deeply embedded in the fabric of the town. They owned Blackthorne, and they punished her for trying to tarnish their family name. She had to keep quiet and ignore everything, promising herself that as soon as she graduated, she'd get a place at a university far from Blackthorne where no one knew her.

Allie wants to shout now, shout anything. Make the world hear her, make everyone know that she has power, even if they've been stonified. Maybe there's a part of them that can still hear, and she needs them to know that she can't be walked all over. That's why she's still here, isn't it? Why the Power's not turned her into a Night Worshipper? Why she's one of the few people in Blackthorne who can still think and speak and act.

But she can't start thinking like that again, believing that people will listen to her. Because they won't—not when there's still an O'Donovan in this town. Even if Riko was out of the picture, she knows how strong the O'Donovan web is. Allie can't put herself through that torment again. It's a miracle the team is talking to her as it is—Kiersten and Dan were both friends with other O'Donovans.

She'd been suspicious of Riko when she'd realized she'd be in his team, thinking he'd continue the bullying. But he didn't. He never mentioned it, just watched her strangely for the first few days, then gave her and Aion the menial jobs, like checking social media.

She and Aion make notes, gathering more and more of the theories various people have come up with. There's still a group going strong who reckon it's a sign of Hell coming to earth. Others think it's something to do with 4G. There's a small outcrop of people who are studying calcification and crystals too, convinced it's linked. Allie doesn't pay much attention to that.

"Do you think it *is* something supernatural?" she asks Aion as they make a quick lunch. She thinks of her night vision and wonders again if Aion has a power. Or if it's just her. She nearly told him once, a couple of days after it all started—but then the witch-hunters came to her street. They lit a house on fire, shouting that the flames would kill the 'witches' among them who were responsible for the stonifications. She and Aion and her father rushed out, as did all the other neighbors who still remained in town, and dowsed the flames with water for hours. Eventually the hunters left, and luckily the sky gave up rain, helped smother the blaze.

And so Allie kept her mouth shut about her power, after all. Sometimes, it feels like she's never allowed to speak in Blackthorne.

"It's ridiculous, people turning to stone," is all Aion says as he shrugs and pushes back his red hair. Allie has always liked his hair. It's the same shade as hers—and it's what bonded the two of them together, back on their first day of primary school.

The truth is, no one knows what is actually going on. And Allie thinks it's pointless, all this research that Riko has their team doing. As if they're going to be the ones to discover the cause of the night worshipping curse and therefore the cure.

ALLIE SAYS SHE'LL walk Aion home. She always does this after their meetings—there's just something comforting about walking through the decimated town with her best friend—and Aion still doesn't know that she never returns straight to her own house after.

She doesn't know why she goes to the O'Donovans' house. She just does. Something draws her over there, and she can't explain it. It's that feeling again—the one that makes her think she's forgotten something huge, something important.

INSIDE THE NIGHT

As she picks her way over to the posher part of town, the part where the houses stand individually with huge driveways and iron gates, Allie keeps an eye on the sky. Sundown isn't for an hour yet. She and Aion worked a little later than normal, and with the nights drawing in earlier and earlier, she'll only have half an hour at the property before she should head back.

A grand sign welcomes her to Meadowview Road. Allie's pace quickens.

There. She sees the house.

Kyle is at the edge of the lawn, and he looks like a guard-dog. He's crouching down a little, like he's about to pick a rose or something from the flower beds.

Allie looks toward the house. There are no lights on inside it. Riko isn't back. He's still out, looking for more survivors, like he does all the time. They never find any more though.

The air is cold—there may even be a frost tonight—and Allie picks her way to her favorite spot in the shrubbery right behind Kyle's statue, shrouded in shadow. Once, Riko was standing by the kitchen window when she was here, and she held her breath when he looked right in her direction. It had still been light and he could've come outside, demanded to know what she was doing, but he didn't. She breathed a sigh of relief when he didn't see her.

Allie doesn't know why she's drawn here almost every day. Why she stares at the statue of the boy she hates. Maybe she's lured here by her subconscious. Because she wants revenge on Kyle for what he did.

The Power's already had its revenge—but it doesn't feel like enough.

She shifts her weight from foot to foot, then looks down. Scattered pebbles lie in front of her feet. She bends to pick one up and feels the weight of it in her hand. It feels good. Allie closes her eyes and imagines herself throwing it at Kyle's statue. Throwing it at his head so hard a crack will appear around his neck and his head will fall off. His skull and face will shatter into a thousand pieces that can never be put back together.

Allie has this urge to behead Kyle every time she's here, but she never acts on it. She relishes in her imaginings of destroying him just as he destroyed her. And if she does, it will be over. Her revenge will be done, gone.

No. She's got to think of a better way to make him pay.

FOUR

The woman has pale skin and pale hair. Her forehead is high and domed, and her eyes are slightly too far apart. She is wearing a long white dress that billows around her hips and legs and clings to the curves of her breasts and the narrowness of her waist, covering her up while showing her womanly form.

Allie stares at the painting on her kitchen wall. It's hers—a painting of Penelope, Odysseus's wife in Homer's *The Odyssey*, from that same art class where Kyle had drawn Medusa. She read the book twice that term, trying to find inspiration, but instead she found herself getting annoyed at how Penelope's whole life revolved around being loyal and faithful to her absent husband. She wanted Penelope to do something of her own accord, something exciting beyond deceiving and tricking the suitors who came looking for her. Even then, she was still no more than 'the faithful wife.'

When Carly saw Allie's painting, she told everyone that Allie must be gay as well as inbred—lumping the two together, as if homosexuality was a crime. Not that Allie particularly minded the inbred accusation either—that just meant she was like Medusa, for Medusa's parents Phorcys and Ceto were siblings. But Carly had said it to be an insult, which cemented Allie's desire for something terrible to happen to her. Something that would make Carly feel weak and helpless and like she didn't matter at all.

Or maybe even something worse. Something that would remove Carly from Allie's life altogether.

Allie stares at her painting of Penelope a lot in the evenings, after she's had a few drinks and a few cigarettes. When the world's becoming a little more hazy around her, when her heartbeat is sluggish. She wonders, as she stares at Penelope's form, if it would be easier if she *was* a lesbian because then people wouldn't keep making jokes when they hear rumors that she's asexual—likening her to a plant because that's the only other time they've really heard the word *asexual*, thanks to biology class. Sometimes Allie wonders if she actually *is* a lesbian even though she's asexual. A website she saw said you can be both.

Allie reaches for her third can of lager. Maybe she's addicted now. An alcoholic. The thought's almost funny, and she laughs, in spite of herself. Her laugh is throaty and low, and it doesn't sound like her. But then again, Allie rarely sounds like herself now. Rarely even looks like herself.

She layers dark makeup around her eyes, and she doesn't take it off to sleep. Her pillow smudges it, making bigger circles appear around her eyes—though maybe those are partly real. There's something comforting about putting makeup on after she's stolen it from the supermarket—though is it stealing, if no one's there to take money now?—as if the act of applying it makes her stronger. Makes her into a different person. Someone who is strong enough to cope with all this, someone who drinks and smokes, someone who can survive the curse, someone who isn't afraid of telling others she's probably asexual and maybe she likes women too. Or maybe she doesn't.

She thinks of Aion.

She likes him—emotionally and intellectually, and yes, he has a nice body. And she appreciates Riko's muscular arms, even though she hates herself for it. So, shouldn't that mean she should feel something else? She doesn't know, and she's too embarrassed to tell anyone.

The clock strikes seven. Allie sighs. It's going to be a long night. Maybe she should get a cat or something. An animal to keep her company at night. Or a dog. Dogs won't want to leave the house at night like a cat might.

Yes, she should get a dog. There are plenty of them roaming the streets now. There used to be a rescue center in town, especially for dogs, but the owners were cursed to stone that first night, and then someone opened the dogs' pens. Let them out. Now, they run free.

Her legs have that jittery feeling in them again, so she gets up to stretch them. The movement makes her bladder spasm and her kidneys hurt. Allie heads to the bathroom and relieves herself, wincing as her bladder pain gets stronger. She stares at the crystals on the shelf above the sink. They almost make her want to laugh.

She and Aion ordered the crystals especially from Greece, maybe six weeks ago, for a summoning spell. She's not sure of the timing—nothing is in order in her head any more—but she knows they ordered the crystals before the stonifications started. Before the Power appeared in the sky. Before the sonic boom.

They'd been reading loads of blogs on summoning gods and convinced themselves they'd be able to summon Medusa. Allie had always believed in magic and mythology as a child, convinced there was a dimension of the world that wasn't visible to her. And she wanted to make Kyle feel pain and fear when he realized Medusa was real. She wanted Kyle to hurt just as he'd hurt her.

Allie was never quite sure whether Aion really believed that a goddess could be summoned. Not like how she did. Maybe he thought her obsession with Medusa was a reaction to the trauma she'd been through, and was just trying to support her. Of course he knew what Kyle had done to her—even if they never talked about it properly because Allie told him she didn't want to.

He knew. Everyone in Blackthorne did. But now, no one speaks of it at all.

Still, whether he believed or not, Aion agreed to summon Medusa in the end, after Allie told him that they could enact revenge on Kyle, the O'Donovans, and even Carly and her gang—everyone who made Aion's life a misery because he'd dared to be friends with Allie. Not to mention get revenge on Kyle for what he'd done to her.

But she and Aion never actually got a chance to try out the spell. It was bizarre—there they'd been, talking of summoning Medusa, and now there was a Medusa-esque power in the sky, turning people to stone. A power that got Kyle pretty quickly. Aion whooped when he heard the news.

Allie swallows hard, dismissing the memory. After washing her hands and then taking more of her medications, she heads downstairs. She grabs a book from the shelf, settles down and—

Something thuds above her head, and Allie freezes, looks up. She watches as a crack appears in the ceiling. Her heart pounds as it spreads across, getting bigger and bigger. A grating sound fills her ears, then the ground's shaking.

Rushing sounds wrap around her, and mugs fly off her draining board.

Run!

The house shakes. Dust fills the air, and the air's gritty, sharp fragments diving down her throat.

The painting of Penelope clatters to her feet.

Get out!

Allie pants, and the room spins. And she's in the lounge now. The front door's ahead of her—but no! She can't go outside.

She mustn't go outside! She—

A beam crashes down. Allie screams. Wood splinters, and stone—so much stone. And a stone hand—her sister's—on the carpet in front of her.

Another beam falls. Something hits the back of her head, and Allie grunts as she falls forward. Her vision goes dark for a moment, but then she's scrambling about. Is it the Power doing this, wanting more victims, hungry when its prey are caging themselves away? Something else? Is there more that can hide inside the night than what she's already seen?

Her hands close on chunks of plasterboard, and she clings to them as if they can save her. She's on her knees, debris pressing through her jeans, painful and sharp.

The ground rumbles, and above her is a creaking sound. She jolts and looks up. The ceiling above— where her bedroom is—is bowing. A high-pitched pop, and then a loud hissing sound fills the air.

Allie smells gas.

Her lungs ache. She looks toward the front door. There's a pathway clear through the debris to it. Her heart pounds.

No! Don't go outside! It's dark!

If she stays here, she's going to be crushed and suffocated.

Allie surges forward, dragging herself to the front porch, and yanks open the door.

FIVE

The darkness has teeth, and the night is trying to eat Allie. Huge welts form on her bare hands and arms, and the darkness is burning her, tearing her skin to shreds. Something wet and slick slides down her arms, and she screams as needles of pain drive into her face.

She blinks frantically, trying to see, but she is panicking, breathing too fast, and she can't stop gulping. Her throat is closing up, and the air feels too thick, too heavy. It's weighing her down and the ground shakes. She falls to her knees on the concrete slabs, drags a hand down the side of her face, leaving a wet trail.

Behind her, her house is falling in at one end. No longer a protective sanctuary. The Power is tearing it apart, and Allie's sure the whole structure's going to come down soon. She concentrates and hones in on the rest of the street; her vision gets brighter, clearer, sharper, and she sees the other buildings crumbling at a much faster rate than her own home.

There is nowhere indoors that is safe.

She looks up at the sky. She cannot see the Power there. But she can feel it. It is greedy. It is taking and taking, and it's not going to stop.

Allie forces herself to her feet and runs. The ground shakes again, and the trees at the end of the road move toward her, swaying. She ducks as a branch flies past her. Her lungs ache and burn and her head spins. She's got to find the others.

Gabe's house is closest, so she heads for Manor Close, the posh part of the town where the physiotherapist lives. She runs and the ground is still moving, and the sky breaks, a booming sound echoing around her, bouncing off the fallen homes.

A dog barks, and Allie sees it, a Labrador cowering by a house that's partly fallen down, only propped up precariously by one pillar. Allie falters a little—should she try and calm the dog? See if it's okay?

But something booms from the sky, and rain soaks her suddenly, blinding her. Her body stutters and ice-cold winds wrap around her. Allie tries to catch sight of the Labrador again, but the water's swirling in the road now, and everything's shaking, and she can't see.

She's got to find the others.

Allie's head pounds as she runs. A fence post flies past, barely missing her. As she races forward, she can't help but imagine it spearing her body, puncturing her lungs. Coldness lassoes her heart.

Broken statues—broken Night Worshippers—are everywhere. A stone head rolls toward her. The person's still smiling. Allie gulps. She doesn't recognize the face. It's not one of her team.

"Mulberry Close . . . Cranmore . . ." She mutters the names of the streets as she passes them. Some have their signs still rooted in the tarmac, some don't, but it doesn't matter. Allie memorized the layout of the town long ago.

At last, just when Allie thinks her heart is going to explode, she reaches Manor Close. It's no different to the estates she's passed: full of wreckage, trees and bricks and stones everywhere. It's just a pile of rubble. Red bricks and chunks of cement and broken window frames. The wind picks up and howls, and the sound of it makes the hairs on the backs of Allie's arms stand on end.

"Gabe!" Allie shouts, her heart pounding as she looks at what should've been number 1 Manor Close. Nausea twists inside her as the wind whips the name from her mouth. She claps a hand to the base of her throat, which stings, as if nature literally snatched something from her throat when it took away her scream.

The rain gets colder, harder, bouncing off the debris. Water runs down the ground, like a river, sweeping away wooden planks and plastic containers. A teddy bear floats by, and Allie hears a laugh. An evil one.

She whips her head around, heart pounding. No one is in sight. She looks up at the sky. Is it the Power? The Power is laughing?

The sound is too close to be the Power. But who else can it be? She is alone. And terrified.

Oh, God. She's going to die.

They're all going to die. This is *it*.

Allie screams her frustration, and it surprises her, the guttural sound that rips from her soul. How animalistic it feels. She's been reduced to nothing but a creature who screams sounds that aren't words, that have no shape other than terror.

A hand sticks out from the rubble by her feet. It looks rubbery and grey. It's stone, not flesh.

The hand is cold. Doesn't move when she touches it.

Allie's heart leaps, and she falls to her knees, bashing her shin on a lump of rock as she moves the rubble from the person's arm, from the person's body.

Then she screams.

It's Gabe, and his face has been smashed in. His skull has broken, and she can see the rough, cracked edges of it. And the brain beneath, mashed up, spilling out beneath his jaw.

Her stomach lurches.

The Power in the sky laughs even harder. It has a female voice. It sounds exactly like Allie, and Allie pretends it doesn't.

Local Suicide Victim Was Pregnant

BLACKTHORNE — The postmortem carried out on the recently-deceased Maliah Swan has revealed the eighteen-year-old schoolgirl was pregnant at the time of her death. The identity of the father of Swan's baby is currently unknown, but there is speculation that the pregnancy was the cause of Swan's decision to end her life.

SIX

"Allie!"

The cry is raw, a knife piercing her insides, and Allie jolts, looks up. She's been running for what seems like hours. She doesn't know how she's still moving, and she can't recognize any of the town now. It's all rubble and broken Night Worshippers and the odd fleeing shadow of a dog, the hiss of a cat.

Two figures hurtle toward her. Her heart jumps. Aion and Riko. People. Relief hugs her and she nearly misses her footing, only manages to right herself at the last moment. A shard of pain squeezes through her ankle.

Allie pants hard as Aion and Riko reach her. Aion wraps her in a hug. He smells of blood, rusty and tangy. His head is bleeding and she feels his blood pressing against her face, sticky and hot.

"All right?" Riko looks her up and down and grabs the knife from his belt—ha, as if that can save him from the Power. Then Allie realizes he's holding the knife against her, as if she's the threat.

"What are you doing?" Aion stares at Riko. "That's Allie! She's not the threat here! We have to stick together."

"I'm not going to hurt you," she mutters, as much as she wants to get revenge on the O'Donovans.

Riko grunts, doesn't look convinced, but he turns the knife away. Allie likes that he is scared of her.

Something howls in the distance. It doesn't sound like a dog.

"Have you seen anyone else?" Riko demands. Light glints off the knife's blade, but Allie can't tell where it's coming from.

"Gabe's dead," she says.

"So's Oliver," Aion grunts.

Ice-cold needles of rain drive down. Allie gasps as they burn her skin. She lifts her arms, trying to protect her face.

"No! Don't!" Aion grabs her hands, pulling them back down.

It takes Allie a moment to realize she'd mimicked a Night Worshipper. Her face stings and she tries to hunker down. The three of them crouch low, together. There's a rushing sound in Allie's ears.

"The castle!" Aion shouts, pointing. "It's the only place still standing!"

Allie looks ahead. The skyline is lit up by the eerie color of the sky—a vibrant purple—and Allie can see the buildings falling as the storm wraps around them, all of them except for the castle. It looks exactly the same, and the storm's angry fingers are leaving it alone.

Blackthorne Castle has been half in ruins for a good few hundred years, but the west side of the castle has been intact for centuries. A few years ago, a historian made a documentary about Blackthorne and it was closed to the public while filming took place. Allie watched that documentary when it aired six months later. The producers and historian had been up at the top of the west tower—the only part that's not open to the public as Health and Safety officers deemed it too dangerous. But it didn't look dangerous in the documentary. The historian, whatever his name was, was lounging about, leaning against the walls. There were no safety ropes anywhere. It was probably just deemed unsafe because of the height. The west tower stretches up for six stories, considerably higher than the main part of the castle that's been crumbling down in slow motion.

"We can't go there!" Riko bellows over the chaos of the storm.

"What?" Allie screams, staring at him.

"We can't!" he yells. There's something in his eyes that doesn't look quite right. "You haven't heard the stories?"

"The stories?" Allie shakes her head. What the hell is he on about? *Of course* they've got to go to the castle—it's the only place the Power isn't ripping apart and they can't stay out here.

"Ghost stories?" Aion frowns at Riko. "You're scared of ghosts?"

Ghosts. Allie wants to laugh.

"No, I just don't like that place." Riko folds his arms, looking defensive as he glances over at Allie quickly before looking away from her.

He doesn't want to go to the castle? Allie frowns. Why? Instinctively, she feels like that is something she should know—but she can't remember. It's that feeling again, that she's forgotten something huge, something really important. But looking at Riko now, the way he's breathing hard and staring anywhere but at her, makes her sure that Riko *does* remember something, knows something she doesn't.

I thought you were dead. Is the Power affecting anyone else's memory?

The howl rises again, closer now, and her skin prickles.

Allie turns to ask Aion if he feels like he's forgotten something too—suddenly overcome with the urge to discuss it—but a dog hurtles through the air, a black streak of fur and teeth, almost hitting them, and once again she's silenced.

"We have to go now!" She grabs Aion's hand. It is surprisingly warm, and she clings to him, suddenly realizing how cold she is. Her own hands are like blocks of ice.

"No, we can't!"

Allie ignores Riko. They'd be stupid not to go.

Allie and Aion hunker down as much as they can as they run. The storm sends daggers of semi-frozen water at them, cutting Allie's face. She feels something thicker than water sliding down the side of her face and tastes rust at the corner of her mouth. Her feet slip on the sodden grass and in the pools of mud and blood several times, but Aion catches her.

Twice, Allie twists her head and looks behind her, trying to see Riko. Because he must be coming with them, right? But the night's too dark and moody, and even when lightning flashes—burning an imprint of her zoomed-in surroundings into her retinas—she can see no other life in the area. Even the dogs and cats have gone. It's just her and Aion, panting, clinging to each other as they run.

They jump over broken statues, and Allie tries not to look at their faces. Mrs. Mack from the bakery. The boy who used to deliver the newspapers, before the Power came. A local farmer. The postmaster.

She tries not to think about Ellie, in the cupboard under the stairs. She wonders if that part of her house is still standing, if somehow the house has managed to protect her sister, even as the Power has ripped down the walls. She thinks of her painting of Penelope, and she imagines it whipping through the vicious air.

"There!" Allie shouts, pointing ahead. Blackthorne Castle. The air around it is completely still.

When Allie steps into the calm pocket of air, into the sanctuary of the castle, something happens inside her head. It's a crawling sensation, like her brain is slowly rotating in her skull, twisting round. Her vision jars and blurs. She sees Aion, the way his dark eyes get lighter—because everything's getting lighter. And she feels terror—terror, remembered. She hears angry male voices—Riko's and Kyle's? She feels hands on her arms, shoving her forward. She shouts—but it's just a choking sound, and the stone wall of inside of the west tower is in front of her. Just a glimpse, before there's bright light, shining as if through a window. The sky. Trees.

A scream.

Then she can see and hear and feel nothing, because there is nothing there. The world disappears, and there's fire in her veins.

Her last thought is that it doesn't matter if she burns up. The castle will protect her—she doesn't know how she knows it, but she does. Because the castle remembers her, and this memory is a promise.

SEVEN

"*You really think you can win against me?*" *Kyle is laughing. "Don't you know who I am?"*

Allie is not laughing. She's scared, her heart is pounding. She stares around the castle tower—her sanctuary. Until he followed her.

She shifts, trying to get Kyle to move away from the wall. She doesn't want him to see the drawings there—her designs, her reclamation of her work. Kyle would recognize them from the painting he plagiarized from her, and then he'd see it as a confrontation, she's sure. Or he'd claim she'd copied him. Or worse—that she admired him, and maybe he'd want to draw on her wall too. And she can't have that. This is her place. Kyle is an intruder.

"What do you want?" she snarls. "Another go?"

"I want you to stop with all these lies," Kyle says.

Her notebooks are spread out on the floor, and Kyle mustn't see them—she mustn't give him more ammunition to hate her, not when she's trying to plan revenge. And where the hell is Aion? He was supposed to be there to help her. They'd planned this carefully, and it had to be now—today was the summer solstice. The date that all the books said was perfect for the summoning.

"I'm not lying," she bites out through gritted teeth.

"But you are." His laugh gets darker, deeper, more sinister. "That's what my family thinks. That's what everyone thinks. And face it, you can't prove anything happened. It's your word against mine."

Allie swallows hard. "Oh, I can prove it."

Kyle takes a step toward her. "No. You won't be able to. Oh, it's a shame it's come to this," he says. "Such a shame."

EIGHT

"*Allie . . .*" a voice whispers. "*Maliah . . .*"

Allie doesn't hear the voice at first. Not properly—she knows it's there, but the words it speaks—her name—don't mean anything to her. She doesn't know where she is. She is . . . somewhere and nowhere and everywhere.

But then she realizes she has a body, because she is hurting. There is pain, everywhere, and she is gasping, trying to breathe the air that's too thick, and the voice won't stop saying her name.

"*Maliah . . . Maliah . . . Maliah!*"

It's a female voice, a woman. She sounds scared.

Allie opens her eyes.

At first, she can't see anything. The world is too bright, too white around her. She blinks and blinks, but then darker shapes appear, and she sees the woman leaning over her. Brown skin and dark hair.

"Allie, oh, thank God," Kiersten whispers, and then she is hugging Allie to her chest and Allie can barely breathe.

Allie doesn't like being touched, but she pulls away from Kiersten after allowing the woman to hug her a bit. She blinks slowly and looks around. Rough stone walls and a dirt floor. They're in the castle, and the air's all strange. It's like something's humming—like the air is full of a pulsing, unseen energy.

"Aion!" She sees him sitting a few feet away, his back to the stone wall. His head is in his hands, but he looks up at Allie when she shouts his name.

A smile flicks across his face.

Allie tries to stand up, and Kiersten helps her. She looks around. It's daylight.

"What . . . what's happened?" She looks up at the sky—it's just visible through a gap in the wall, up near the ceiling. She can see a beautiful blue color. "Is it just us three?"

Kiersten shakes her head. "Helen and Dan are just outside. We can't go far."

"What?"

Allie pushes her way toward the window. She looks out and her heart thumps. Helen and Dan are both standing a few feet away. The air is still and calm around them, but it is like the castle's in a dome of sorts, something to protect it. Because beyond Helen and Dan, the air is dark and the storm is still going. Chunks of wood and debris fly through the air in swirling patterns. Rain is battering down and the clouds are dark, furious, angry.

"How is this . . ." Allie trails off as she turns to look at Kiersten. The nurse looks tired. Exhausted. Huge circles hang under her eyes.

"We don't know," Kiersten says.

"The castle's protecting us," Aion says.

Is the protection the energy she can detect, that humming?

Aion pulls himself up slowly, grimacing. The cut on his head looks deep, nasty. He joins Allie by the window, nods at her. "Riko didn't follow us."

Riko.

It was his hands on her upper arms. His scream. His touch. And Kyle's. The threats, the tower, the window, the fall.

They were both here. With her. Before. According to that . . . whatever it was, before she passed out. A fragment of a vision, a memory? Could it have been real?

Allie swallows hard and looks outside. There are no signs of anyone. She looks around again, taking note of everyone not here. Everyone who they know is dead or will be dead. Riko. Gabe. Vera. Oliver.

"We're trapped in here?" she asks, feeling a sense of relief despite herself. She couldn't protect her sister, but insisting she and Aion come here was a good idea. At least she's kept him safe.

Kiersten nods. "Seem to be. Dan tried to get out, but it's some sort of forcefield. Burnt his arm badly."

Allie nods like she understands, like all of this makes sense, but it doesn't. "How can the castle be safe from all . . .this?"

"We don't know," Aion says.

Allie nods again. "I'm going to look around."

The others don't stop her and no one volunteers to go with her, not even Aion, so Allie walks into the west tower. A year ago, she photographed it with Aion for a project—that was the first time they'd been to the castle, even though they'd lived in the town all their lives. But it was nearly always a monetized tourist attraction.

She and Aion sneaked through the barriers late one evening. She remembers running her hands over the cold, sand blocks, the callouses on her skin catching on the rough textures.

It looks the same, and it reminds her of all the time and she and Aion spent secretly in the castle thereafter. It was their special place, for just the two of them, until their space was violated.

They grab her, knocking her notebooks and crystals flying, and she screams. She's kicking and punching, trying to hurt them, but they lift her up easily, lift her toward the window.

"No!" she screams. "Please, I'll do anything!"

But neither brother's listening. Each has a steely, glazed-over look in their eyes, and she screams and begs. She shoves back, but they're stronger. Of course they're stronger. They're male and big and tall. Rugby players. They haul her up to the open-window-space. No glass left. Just an empty square space in the stone.

"Please!" Tears run down her face and her fingers scrape against the rough stone. She tries to get a hold on the stone, but she can't. "Please, please!"

They shove her out and Allie falls.

Allie gasps at the . . .memory. It doesn't make sense—doesn't link up with anything before or after. It's just there, floating untethered. Like it has no rightful place in her mind.

She shakes her head. She didn't fall from the tower. She'd have had injuries. She'd have remembered that—and surely Aion would've mentioned it. If he'd been late to meet her at the tower, when they were planning on summoning Medusa, and he'd found her lying on the ground outside, he'd definitely have said something. No, this is just her imagination trying to trick her.

She climbs the tower to the second floor, touching the stones that curve around the wall of the spiral staircase, as if the mere act of touch can ground her. She breathes deeply, and looks closer at the stone.

It's the same as the statues. It looks . . .the same? And it feels the same too—Allie feels connected to both.

But don't all rocks look the same? She shakes away that question and pushes through the doorway onto the second floor. The floor looks solid enough for the most part. Wood. She tests it cautiously at first, she doesn't want two broken legs on top of all this, but it holds.

The energy, that hum, is getting stronger.

She makes her way around the circular room slowly. The air is damp, musty, and she wrinkles her nose. Her lungs do a hitching, panicking thing, and suddenly she wants a cigarette. But of course she hasn't got any with her. Her pack of cigarettes was on her kitchen table.

Tears come to her eyes, and she knows it is silly to cry over cigarettes when the world is ending—because it must be—but she can't help it. She lets the tears fall, lets them blur her vision until she can't see the walls with the coppery serpent designs and—

She jolts.

Serpents? The serpents she drew, way before Kyle stole her art.

Allie drags the back of her hand across her eyes, wiping away her tears. She leans in closer. The wall's a foot away, and she stares at the tower walls, at the designs etched on them. Some of them are carvings, some are painted on.

She expects something to happen when she touches the crude drawings with her fingers, tracing their shapes, but nothing does.

"Allie? You in here?"

Aion's voice makes her jump. She hadn't heard him approach.

She turns to see him entering the room. His arms are stretched out in front of him, like he's feeling his way. Or like he's a zombie.

"Yeah," she says.

Aion moves toward her uncertainly, and Allie grabs his hand. He flinches a little.

"What?" she says, self-conscious.

"Your skin feels weird. Too cold and like rubber."

"Oh." She doesn't know what to say to that, so she pulls him forward. "Look at the snakes," she says, looking back at the wall in front of her. She knows they're important—because they're connected to *the before*.

"What?" Aion squints. "I can't see a thing."

Allie realizes there is no window—no window in the tower.

So she can't have been thrown from it?

She frowns.

"Allie, can you see in the dark?" Aion asks.

She jolts. She must've been using her vision power. And that realization makes her feel weird, like she's working with the Power in the sky that's taken away everything she's ever known. That's killed her sister and father, her friends, her teachers. Her life as she knew it.

"Wait a sec," he says, and then he's pulling out his phone. He flicks the flashlight on, and then raises his eyebrows as he sees the serpents.

"I can't remember it all, Aion," she says. "I mean, I know I drew these here, but . . ." Her words are fast, tumbling out of her. Allie knows this is important, suddenly she's surer of that than she's been about anything before.

"That's not your drawing. That's Kyle's. They're the same as Riko's tattoos," Aion says, sounding confused. "Kyle's been here—to our place?"

Kyle's drawings? What? Allie frowns. No, they were *her* drawings first. And she drew these ones! But then as she tries to remember drawing them, the memory disappears. It's just gone. It doesn't make sense.

"Something's not right," she says, and although her memory of drawing the serpents has gone, the rest of it hasn't—it's just like one piece of the jigsaw has been removed and the other pieces rearranged to seamlessly fill its place. Because everything else is still there. Kyle and Riko, throwing her from the window.

Only the window's not there.

Allie's mind spins, and she feels sick now thinking about Riko. What if that part of her memory *is* real? And somehow the window got filled in? What if they did both hurt her—and that's why Riko didn't want her to go back to the tower, in case it triggered her memory . . . and why he didn't come, himself?

No . . . it can't be. Can it?

"Hey, what's going on?" Kiersten calls up. "You two okay?"

"Come up here," Allie shouts back. Her voice wavers. Everything seems too dangerous, too uncertain now, like the past is being rewritten around them, and she wants to keep what remains of their group together, as if she can protect them.

"We've found something," Aion shouts back.

Their steps on the stone stairs echo and pound through Allie's skull as she waits for the rest of their team to enter the room. The wooden floor creaks threateningly. Dan has a flashlight with him, a big industrial thing, and Helen looks delighted when she sees the drawings, calls them cave art.

"It's the same as Riko's tattoos, right?" Aion says.

When they nod, Aion's explaining about Kyle. Well, not everything—he doesn't talk about what

Kyle did to Allie, or how the whole town tried to ostracize Allie because of it. It's almost like by not mentioning it, Aion is rewriting history so it didn't happen.

But it *did* happen, Allie knows that. She claws at her face, listening to Aion drone on about how Kyle was obsessed with snakes, drawing them everywhere, using the style he copied from her Medusa painting.

"The energy's stronger in this room," Allie says. "It's just . . . vibrating with it."

"Energy?" Dan frowns.

"Can't you feel it?" she asks. "And Riko didn't want Aion and me coming here. Even though it's the only safe place. He chose not to come with us."

She's sure she's right—this must be because he remembers what happened—what he and Kyle did. Whatever's happened to all their memories since the Power came, his is less affected. The first moment he saw that she was in his team, he'd said she thought she was dead. Then he'd looked doubtful, hadn't he? And asked if anyone else's memory was affected.

And now her memory is healing. The energy in the castle has to be what's causing her to remember.

But there's no window in the west tower. So how can her memories be real?

"I can't feel any energy," Helen says. "But I don't like it, all the same. And those snake drawings are creepy. Let's go back downstairs." She moves toward the doorway, but then something flashes. Light, in the room.

Helen screams, and Allie turns, heart pounding.

Power floods through the doorway in waves, and the snakes on the walls are moving. Allie lets out a scream.

Roaring sounds fill the air. And then the energy is growing, increasing. Allie can feel it. It's swamping her, swamping them all.

The energy takes on a visual form. It's a woman's face. A heart-shaped face, large eyes, and snakes for hair. It's just her face, her head. Like she's been beheaded. Like the fallen statues Allie saw as she ran through the town on her way here.

"What the fuck?" Dan makes a choking sound, and Allie's head whips toward him. He can see the energy too? Even though none of them could feel it?

"It's Medusa!" Aion breathes. "Don't look at her!"

Allie's body jolts. Pain flickers around her kidneys as she stares at the woman. She *does* look like Medusa. And Allie is looking at her, but she's not turning to stone. So this can't be the Gorgon . . . only Allie knows deep in her heart that it is.

"Oh my god," she whispers. "What if Kyle and Riko summoned Medusa somehow?"

Could it be possible? Kyle *was* studying Medusa, and he *was* drawing the snakes, and then Riko had the snakes on his arms too. And he didn't want to come here . . .

Everyone stares at the woman's head, even though Aion said to look away. It's suspended a foot in front of the doorway. About twice the size of an actual human head. The snakes writhe and wriggle. Her face looks hard, like it's made of red rock.

But as Allie watches, cracks appear. They run from the corners of the woman's eyes, down her cheeks, like teardrops, until they get to her mouth. The rock around her lips crumbles as Allie watches.

"We warned you this could happen," she whispers, and her words are coldness and ice and anger. *"There were never any guarantees."*

A high-power wave of energy blasts out from the disembodied head. It slows, shimmering in the air, turning everything golden.

Allie screams, turning. Aion grabs her hand and pulls her to him. Kiersten flies across the room as the wave hits her.

Then the wave hits Helen and Dan. It doesn't throw them like it did Kiersten. It wraps around them.

They're petrified in an instant, and the rock mask of Medusa falls—discarded, because Medusa no longer holds onto it. Medusa is free now, and Allie watches as she rejoins the Power in the sky.

For a second, Allie sees the truth: the Power isn't one amorphous entity—it consists of several Gorgons and their energies, all staring down at her. And she's staring back, her chest feeling light and fluttery and her throat too thick, trying to take it all in, before the images are whisked away, and it's just the Power again.

NINE

"So, you think Riko and Kyle summoned Medusa, and now she's destroying the world?" Aion frowns, then nudges Dan's arm with his foot. Completely solid. "Do you realize how crazy this sounds? That's just Greek mythology. This is ridiculous."

"Um, but we had that plan to summon Medusa?" Allie says. Aion never said it was ridiculous then.

Aion's frown deepens. "What?" He shakes his head, disbelief written all over his face. "What are you on about?"

"You've forgotten?" She stares at him, a twisting sensation in her chest. "We talked about this right after the first stonifications happened! You know, how weird a coincidence it was that we were trying to summon her, and we didn't do it—but now people are being turned into stone."

He gives her an odd look. "Why would we want to summon Medusa?"

"For revenge on Kyle!" Her voice rises and she's aware of the look Kiersten's giving her—like she's mad.

Aion frowns more deeply still. "Revenge on Kyle? What for?"

What for?

Allie's gut twists. He doesn't remember? She swallows hard and stares down at the stone forms of Dan and Helen. Her head pounds.

Kiersten clears her throat. "Never mind that right now. There has to be a way to stop this."

Allie wonders if Kiersten remembers what the O'Donovans did to her, if she remembers how Allie had tried to expose that family for what they were. She wants to ask. But how can she, when both of them are looking at her like she's lost her mind?

"Wouldn't it be Riko and Kyle stopping it? Reversing it? If they're the ones that started it?" Aion says, going along with Kiersten.

Allie turns away. She doesn't want to see the statues' open eyes. "And they're both probably dead." She imagines Riko lying somewhere, stone head smashed in just like Gabe's was.

Her gut squeezes. Now that she's remembered the truth, she hopes Riko is as dead and stone-cold as Kyle. As all the O'Donovans.

But is it really true? There's no window in the tower, after all. And Aion and Kiersten don't remember a thing.

Maybe she's going mad after all.

She makes her way to the doorway—all that remains of Medusa is a crumbly red mess on the floorboards—and looks out the window on the stairwell. The storm is still raging, shredding everything beyond their bubble. She doubts anything could survive out there.

Allie's skin prickles. She's staring at the red dust on the floor, the remains of Medusa's mask. She wants to run her hands through it, let it pour from between her fingers, but she doesn't know why. And it would look weird, so she doesn't do it.

"Can you get a phone signal?" Kiersten is asking Aion when Allie returns to the room. "We should try phoning someone. Someone could rescue us. The army, maybe. They've got helicopters."

"They wouldn't get through the storm. And why would they even come for us now? We all chose to stay in Blackthorne."

"But they need to know we're alive," Kiersten says.

"No signal." Aion shrugs. "So that's that idea out the window."

"Then we have to look for somewhere with signal," Kiersten says.

"Go out *there*?" Are you mad?" Aion's face reddens. He shakes his head at Kiersten. "No. We're not leaving here."

"But we can't survive in here. We've got no food," Kiersten says. "No water." She glances at Allie. "Have you got any of your meds with you?"

Allie shakes her head.

"We've got to go back out there." Kiersten looks determined.

Allie makes a noncommittal noise. In her head, Medusa's words echo: *We warned you this could happen. There were never any guarantees.*

Who had the Gorgon been talking to? And what had they done?

"We could look for Riko too," Allie offers. "In case he's still alive."

They do need to find Riko—if he summoned Medusa, he's got to know how to reverse it. But more than that, she wants to demand the truth from him.

She wants to know what happened to her, and she thinks he is the key.

"The storm can't be everywhere. Maybe we can run for it," Kiersten says. "Get out of this town."

THE O'DONOVANS' HOUSE is a mess. It doesn't even look like a house—none of the houses do. But this one seems more of a mess, and Allie is pleased about that.

She stares at the ripped curtains that peek out from the pile of wood and bricks. Plastic rubbish litters the area, swirling round and round in the icy wind. Twice, a garbage bag hits her in the face.

But Allie finds something, a book. A notebook, bound in red leather. It's the only thing that appears to be intact, and it's just sitting on the ground. The storm isn't touching it, just like the storm isn't touching the castle.

She picks up the book. It's heavier than she expected. Her fingers are icy, cramping up, and she nearly drops it. Her breaths almost still completely as she opens it and stares at the drawings and notes and annotations on summoning Gorgons. Something about them is familiar. Too familiar. It makes her stomach twist.

"Look at these drawings." She shows the book to Aion and Kiersten. "Medusa, Stheno, and Euryale," she says, reading the neat scrawl. It's not like how she remembers Kyle's writing, and it's not Riko's either, but it *is* familiar, though she can't place it. "The three Gorgon sisters," Allie breathes.

Allie thinks of her own sisters. Ellie was a year older than Allie, and Sarah three years older than Ellie. As much as Allie wanted to be close to Sarah, she wasn't. Not like she was with Ellie. And for some reason that makes her feel bad now. She didn't take the chance when she had it. Not properly with either of her sisters—just look at the argument she'd had with Ellie the last time she'd seen her. And now both of her sisters are gone, and Allie is sure she's never going to see either of them again. Not alive.

"He's summoned *three* of them?" Aion looks aghast. "This just gets better and better. All this time he's been telling us to find the cause, and it was *him*?"

"Wait." Kiersten holds up her hands. "Why would he summon Medusa and her sisters? It makes no sense."

"Aion told you," Allie says. "Kyle was obsessed with snakes. And power. He and Riko must've summoned Medusa together. It all fits."

Aion grabs the book from her. "Maybe there's something in here about reversing it."

The three of them search and search but there's nothing in the notebook about reversal and they can't find any more notebooks. The night has destroyed whatever else there was.

"Blood offerings?" Allie suggests after a while. "Whenever a sacrifice is needed in films, it's always blood. People cut their palms, don't they?"

That will bring Medusa back, at the least, won't it? And Allie wants to speak to Medusa again. She feels a connection to her.

Medusa is strong. Her position as the Power has proved she's her own weapon, and no one controls her. Allie wants to help Medusa and she wants Medusa to help her.

Aion nods. "Okay. There's a knife downstairs."

"It's Dan's," Kiersten says, her voice shaking.

Ten minutes later, the three of them cut their palms in turn. When it's Allie's turn, her skin seems to be tougher than the others' and her blood is strange, all thick and congealed, in clots. Kiersten looks horrified as she sees it, but she doesn't say anything, because they're trying to do a sacrifice, so they all just wait with their blood dripping.

Nothing happens.

"Maybe it needs to be in the castle—maybe in front of Medusa, or what remains of her. Or in front of all three sisters if all three have been involved in this?" Allie shudders.

"Or maybe it needs to be Riko's blood," Aion mutters. "Maybe *we* can't stop this."

Kiersten frowns. "Riko donated blood—he was always going on about how wonderful he was because of that. Lording it over those who didn't or couldn't."

"So, there'll be some of his blood somewhere?"

"At the hospital," Kiersten says. "We can take a look. Then do all the blood sacrifices together, back at the castle."

"Sounds like a plan," Aion says.

Allie doesn't say anything.

THE THREE OF them break into the hospital. Not that it's breaking in. They just walk in. No one to stop them.

Kiersten knows where they're going, so Allie and Aion follow. They get the blood and Kiersten finds some antibiotics for Allie. Not the right ones though. But Allie barely notices this or considers the implications for her kidneys. She's too preoccupied by the sight and smell of the hospital rooms. The places where the doctors should be, where they were when they talked her through her decision to have an abortion.

She'd never realized there were so many abortion methods. She thought she'd just book into a clinic and that would be it. But the doctors wanted to talk and talk and talk. She didn't want counseling. She just wanted it to be over with. The longer it went on, the longer she waited, the more people would find out.

And they did find out. Her father spitting furious words at her, not believing her when she tried to tell him what had happened, saying it was all her fault. Kyle calling her a slag, laughing, until he realized she was serious when she said she would go to the police, that she'd tell everyone, that she could prove it all. And then he saw only one option, and of course he had the perfect family to help him.

Allie had no one. Not really—because although Ellie had tried to comfort her in secret at first, she couldn't stand up to the O'Donovans publicly, not if she didn't want to lose her job at the factory. Even the bloody factory was owned by them. And one of them must've said something to Ellie, because next thing Allie knew, her sister was telling her to be quiet about her 'story.'

The O'Donovans even took her sister from her.

Lost in memories and miserable, she slips on something wet on the hospital floor, surges forward and—

She falls from the tower, screaming. She tries to turn, mid-air. Above her, leaning out the window of the west tower, the faces of Kyle and Riko O'Donovan are the last things she sees before her body slams into the ground. A moment of pain—thick, excruciating, suffocating pain—and then nothing.

Allie jolts back to the present, breathing hard.

"You okay?" Kiersten asks her.

Allie nods.

But she's not. Not in the slightest.

Kyle and Riko . . . They killed her. Only—she's alive.

TEN

Her head pounds. None of this makes sense. She doesn't know what to think. And she feels . . . nothing. She's just empty.

On autopilot, she and Aion follow Kiersten out of the hospital and back toward the tower, passing her house on the way. She stops when she sees it—the only house on the street that is still partly standing. Everyone else's has been flattened.

Where her father's statue once stood is only wreckage. But she doesn't care about him. Not after the hateful words he spewed at her when she needed a parent most. When she was traumatized and scared and alone and had gone to him for help—only to be shunned.

She just looks for her sister—because suddenly rescuing Ellie is the most important thing. She's got to make sure her sister's okay. She has to.

Aion tries to stop her, but Allie ignores him. She steps over broken timbers and shards of glass and wires—so many wires, green and red, with exposed ends—and steps inside the ruin of her house. It reminds her of Blackthorne Castle, how part of that is in ruins but part is standing. Her house is the same.

Allie reaches the cupboard under the stairs—jagged plasterboard and peeling paint and broken wood. But the cupboard is still there. *Ellie* is still there.

She drags her sister behind her, out of the wreckage of their half-surviving home. It's difficult, and her kidneys are hurting, and she's lightheaded. Hell, it's not even fair that her kidneys still hurt her. Isn't that supposed to stop when you die?

Then she reminds herself that this isn't Hell. This is real. Somehow, she's still alive. So she survived the fall?

But she didn't. She's sure of it.

She plows on, dragging Ellie. Neither Aion nor Kiersten offer to help her.

But she doesn't need them. She will protect her sister.

THEY TRY WITH Riko's blood first, using the flashlight on Aion's phone. They drip the blood onto the floor of the west tower room. Allie finds herself wishing it was Kyle's blood they had as well. She wants to see both of them on the floor, weak and pathetic.

She'd have liked to see Kyle's transformation into stone. See the look of sheer terror on his face. She'd have reveled in it.

Still, his brother is the next best thing, and Allie is not careful with his blood.

"What's up with you?" Aion asks her, glancing at her strangely.

Allie realizes she's frozen to the spot. She's staring at the place where the window had been—that crude space, she remembers, with no glass. She blinks and heat flushes through her and she sees herself being forced through there by Riko and Kyle. Thrown from the window—by her murderers.

Murderers.

"Allie?" Aion's voice gets louder.

Allie shakes her head. "When did it happen?" she murmurs, and she's counting on her fingers, trying to work it out.

Kiersten stands behind Aion, looking confused.

Allie keeps counting. "A month ago . . .?" Was that when she . . . died?

"What? Just before the stonifications started?" Aion says. "What are you talking about?"

Allie points at where the window should be. Shivers work through her body. "I . . ."

"Come on, just make a circle with the blood," Kiersten says, and Allie realizes she is holding Riko's blood still. It's in a transfusion bag, she can see that, but she can't shake the way it feels like his actual blood is touching her.

Her *murderer* is in her hands.

"Make a circle with it," Kiersten says again.

Allie makes a circle with it while her gut churns.

"Or a star?"

She makes a very wonky star with it, and she gets some of it on her hands. She doesn't like that. Doesn't like the thought that one of the O'Donovan brothers is still touching her.

"Maybe it needs our blood too—as we're the ones trying to reverse it?" Aion says.

Allie doesn't wince as the blade slices open her palm. She barely even feels the pain. She can't think of anything but her murder—because she *was* murdered. She is sure.

Nothing happens. Maybe they're not doing it right. Maybe they need to say the magic words.

A snort rises in Allie's throat. This isn't a fairy tale where magic words will save them all.

This isn't a fairy tale at all.

"Try dripping the blood onto the notebook," Kiersten suggests.

"Or onto Medusa." Allie indicates the crumbled remains. She doesn't like looking at the small pile of rubble just off-center of the doorway. They need to bring her back here, talk to her, find a way to stop the stonifications, help each other.

The light from Aion's phone dims and flickers as they drip the blood on Medusa's old mask. Allie grits her teeth. Will this do it? Will this be enough?

"Please," she whispers, and her voice is strange. It's pleading and it's begging and it's desperate, because she's tired now. So tired suddenly. "I need to know what happened." And Medusa will tell her, won't she?

Her kidneys are hurting more, enough for her to cry, and it's not fair that she's still got their pain when all this is going on, when . . .

A loud thud fills the room. Allie jumps, turns.

The tower shakes. It's falling. The storm's gotten into the bubble. It's not safe.

Cold air whips around her.

"Run!"

They all scurry, and Allie tries to grab Ellie, tries to bring her with them, but her sister's hand breaks off in hers. She runs, holding onto Ellie's fingers, clenching them close to her chest and—

INSIDE THE NIGHT

The wall of the castle blows out. Power erupts from the sky, and someone's howling.

No, *Euryale* is howling. Allie doesn't know how she knows it's her—the second oldest of the Gorgon sisters—but she does.

And Allie can't breathe. Her lungs are on fire, and she trips, falls—only she doesn't fall. Something catches her, the air catches her, the sky catches her, and she is up there and down here at once. Her soul is in two, three, four pieces. No, more. She is everywhere, and she looks over the town of Blackthorne, looks over the whole of Devon, of England, as she searches for people. Because man needs to pay. Man *has* to pay. That was the deal.

The deal? Allie blanches. But it's there in her mind—a foggy scene where the gods were there, around her, and she was broken, flying free and desperate.

"It's you . . ." Aion's voice wobbles, and he points at Allie, and she's back on the ground again. She's outside the tower, and her breaths aren't right, and she can't remember getting there. She doesn't know what is happening, and it scares her more than anything— more even than being in the tower room with Kyle and Riko.

Riko. The man she invited into her house. Her team's leader. Allie turns—in her human body—and throws up sour, stringy bile. She wipes it from her mouth, tries to flick away the long stringy pieces of it that stick to her fingers.

Kiersten is shrieking, and Allie wishes she wouldn't.

And Allie looks up and realizes that the face in the sky *is* her face. She is looking in a mirror, and it *is* her up there. What the hell?

"You're Medusa!"

Somewhere to her right, Aion's voice is full of disbelief, and Allie is staring at herself in the sky. Just her head. Beheaded. Her snakes are angry.

She's really dead.

Fury fills her and she turns, heading down from the tower, for the O'Donovans' property. Her muscles ache and burn, but the ache is good. It's pain. It means something is going to happen.

"Allie!" Aion shouts after her. "Allie, what's going on?"

But Allie doesn't answer—because power is flooding through her. Power that connects her to herself in the sky, to Medusa. She *is* Medusa. And she remembers.

ELEVEN

"*Maliah? Maliah, you need to wake up.*"

A twisting sensation pulls through Allie as she opens her eyes. At first, she can't see anything. There's just darkness, and she's not sure she even is awake. Is alive—because she remembers plummeting from the tower window, remembers the fall, remembers the crack through her spine, the pain in her legs, and arms—and then nothing more.

"Maliah, you need to see us."

The words twist inside Allie, awakening her senses. She feels small twigs digging into her back and something cold and hard beneath her left hand. The back of her head feels wet and sticky. Slowly the darkness lifts, moving at the corners first, like there's a square blanket over her and just the corners are being lifted.

But then the whole blanket disappears, and her vision is pixelated. A dark mass over her, moving, squirming, as the pixilation clears.

Medusa's severed head hangs above her. Just the head—stopping right below her jaw. No neck. Allie can see the vertebrae of Medusa's spine, the one anchoring onto the skull. Tissue and sinews hang down.

Allie screams—but only a squeak comes out. She tries to sit up, but she cannot move.

Her body . . .

Her eyes widen—or at least she thinks they do. She sees the tower above her, behind Medusa's head. The window looks even higher. Riko and Kyle are long gone.

"I am here as requested," Medusa says. "Now that the final piece of the summoning has been completed."

Requested? The final piece?

Allie frowns. Then she remembers her notebooks, the incantations, the spells she was trying to do in the tower—because she wanted revenge on Kyle. Only then he turned up. He laughed at her, called her names, and then his brother arrived. She's abandoned the spell . . . and it needed the final bit to be cast still.

Someone must've done it.

A strange feeling brushes over her soul. She looks back up at the window, and sees a face. Aion. He's crying.

"He completed the summoning for you," Medusa whispers.

"*What? Can he see me?*" *Allie nearly chokes. She doesn't want her best friend to see her like this.*

"*You are not really here, Maliah. They removed your body two weeks ago.*"

"*My body? They all think I'm dead.*"

"*You are. And the papers printed what the O'Donovans paid them to—or at least they did at first. Now, what do you want most of all right now?*" *Medusa whispers.* "*I want to help you. I recognize myself in your soul, and we never turn our back on a sister.*"

As she speaks, Medusa's snakes radiate out from her head, like a peacock's tail. And behind Medusa, Allie sees the Gorgons. Two of them. Monstrous women with snakes for hair.

"*Stheno and Euryale,*" *Allie breathes.*

The three Gorgon sisters smile.

"*We have contacts, we can get you whatever you want, Maliah, but you have to say it now. Time is running out.*"

Allie looks up at the beautiful creatures. "*I want to go back. I want all of this to have never happened. Aion can't think I'm dead!*"

"*Cronus and the Fates owe us,*" *Euryale says.* "*They can rewrite the timestream and correct the life thread.*"

"*Cronus?*" *Medusa says.* "*The God of Time? No. He is destructive. We need Aion, the god of eternity.*"

Aion? Allie thinks of her best friend.

"*Aion does not owe us,*" *Euryale says.* "*And seeking him out would alert others of what we are trying to do—they'd stop us.*"

Medusa's eyes fix onto Allie. "*Very well. We can try, but Cronus craves chaos. We cannot guarantee time and life will resume as you know it.*"

Hope surges within Allie. She just has to be alive again—she can't have let the O'Donovans win. "*That's fine!*" *It wasn't like life as she'd known it had been so great, anyway.*

"*Is there anything else you want?*" *Medusa asks.*

"*Revenge,*" *Allie says.* "*I want revenge.*"

"*Then this shall be revenge,*" *Medusa says, and Allie feels no more.*

TWELVE

The ground beneath her feet rumbles with every step Allie takes, and the sky cracks. A bolt of lightning shoots down and grabs a sliver of the horizon. Hissing sounds fill the air.

But with every step she takes, she gets stronger, more and more power flowing through her veins. The power of Medusa, who she's merged with. The power of Cronus, the god of time, who must've bent the timestream for her. The power of the Fates who brought her back.

The sign for Meadowview Road is lying down, broken clean in two. Adrenaline pounds through her as she makes her way to number thirty-one.

There. She sees Riko.

He is frozen to the spot, just outside the front door—the frame is still standing, and the door's hanging off its hinges slightly. With a smile, she realizes he's reaching for the door handle. A task he never completed.

Good. Look at how much *she* never completed.

She doesn't need him—not for answers, not as her leader. She knows what happened now, and who's to blame.

And she will make them pay.

Kyle's still by the flower bed, but Allie runs at Riko's statue first. She slams his stone body into the doorframe, shattering his right arm.

She doesn't know if the stonified bodies can feel pain, but even if they can, it doesn't matter. Riko hasn't suffered nearly enough.

She grabs him, hauling him up, struggling under his weight, then shoves him back down. He doesn't break.

Allie lets out a guttural scream, her fury unleashing more and more power. Above her, the sky crackles, and she looks up—sees her face up there. The snakes on her head whip about in the sky, getting bigger and bigger, elongating until they're reaching down to the earth, down to Allie.

She doesn't know how she does it, but she controls the snakes, directs them to slither under Riko's broad shoulders, under his waist, his legs. The snakes lift him up.

"Higher!" Allie hisses, watching as the statue gets smaller and smaller above her. until he's small enough and got the farthest to fall. "Now!" she screams.

The snakes throw Riko down.

He lands in the rubble, shattering, throwing dust and grit against Allie's seeping eyeballs, but she doesn't blink. She doesn't do anything. She just watches the cracks as they run across his body.

And when the dust has settled and the snakes have returned to the sky, she turns her attention to Kyle.

"It's your turn, *baby*," she whispers, making her way toward him. And it's not fair that he's made of stone, because she wants him to flinch. She wishes he'd been able to see what she just did to Riko. She wants him to feel fear.

She wants revenge.

Allie grabs a handful of gravel. It's laced with broken pieces of glass and they stab her fingers, but she doesn't feel the pain, just stares at the streams of crimson from her hand, how they run in rivulets over the pebbles. It doesn't look right. Then she shakes her head, shakes all that away, and focuses on the one thing she's always wanted to do since Kyle hurt her.

With the power of Medusa flowing into her, Allie flings the gravel at Kyle's statue. She flings the gravel harder and harder, scraping more of it off the ground. There. She chips Kyle's eye. Satisfaction fills her, and it swells inside her, pulses to get out, to expand.

And Allie lets it, lets it drive her.

She looks toward the pile of rubble that is the house. Her eyes fall on a broken bit of wood. Within seconds, it's in her hands. Feels a good weight.

She strikes Kyle's body over and over again.

"Allie! What are you doing?"

It's Aion's voice. He grabs her, and Allie shouts at him, tries to push him away, but he doesn't back off.

"No!" she screams, whirling around with her weapon.

Aion's eyes widen. He's breathing hard, panting. There's a new cut on his face. A snake of red weaving down his right cheek. Crimson on white.

"What are you doing? Allie—what the hell is going on?"

She tries to turn back to Kyle's shattered body, but Aion gets in the way. Annoyance fills her. Does he think she won't hit him?

Then she startles—where did that thought come from? That wasn't her . . . that was . . . She looks up at the sky. Was it one of them? A Gorgon putting her thoughts inside Allie?

She'd never hurt Aion. He's her friend—her only one.

But she has work to do.

"Get away, I need to finish this." Her voice is a hiss.

"It was you?" He stares at her. "You summoned Medusa?"

"No! *You* did—you finished the summoning," Allie says. "You don't remember, but it's true."

Aion's eyes widen. "But how . . . You're her. You're Medusa. How is this possible? Why don't I remember?" Confusion and anger battle to win his face. "Allie! Why aren't you speaking? Answer me!"

Her heart beats heavier, and she looks up at the sky. The Medusa face—her face—is watching. She sees herself blink up there, and then just for a moment, she is up there too. Her soul in that body, and she's looking down. Down at the hundreds and thousands of towns and cities in England that she's taken out her revenge on.

This is what her enhanced night vision is good for. To see the havoc she's wreaked.

To see her revenge. To see how it spread beyond the men she meant it for.

"Allie?" It's Kiersten's voice.

Allie snaps back into her body—the rotting corpse—and jolts toward Kiersten, in shock. Power floods from her hand and fires out toward the older woman. It hits Kiersten in the chest, and Kiersten makes a small noise of surprise. Then her hands turn gray. Stone. Allie watches as the stone spreads.

"What the hell?" Aion's voice shakes. He is looking at Allie—pure fear on his face now. He backs away slowly, his hands held up. "Why are you doing this? Kiersten's our friend."

"I didn't mean to," Allie whispers, horrified. "It was an accident."

She looks down at her hands, ashamed—and then her skin begins to change. It's forming welts, and then it's splitting, and her flesh—rotten and swollen—is bursting out from under the skin. She is a monster, just as Athena made Medusa into a monster all those years ago, punishing her for the crime Poseidon had committed against her.

Allie looks at her body, her rotting carcass. At her face in the sky. Then back at her friend. He's staring at her, revulsion on his face—and she can't blame him. He takes a step back, then another one and another one. Trying to get as far away from her as possible.

Allie starts to reach out to him, and he retreats even further.

"No! I'm your friend! You're not doing that to me! I'm your only friend, Allie."

She's still reaching for him, and she realizes what he thinks. That she'd hurt him. And it reminds her of the thought she had earlier—that she *could* hurt him. But, no, he's her best friend. He was there for her—even if he doesn't remember everything. They have to stick together.

"Aion, I . . ." Her words get stuck in her throat. She feels strange. With Kyle and Riko dead—one smashed now by her hand, the other cracked and chipped—she expected to feel better. Freer. But she doesn't. Because she thinks of everyone else. She looks around. She can see the other statues on Meadowview Road. So many people.

Her family. Her own sister. Her father. Her chest hitches.

She's responsible for all of this.

"Why, Allie?" Aion demands.

Her fingers start to shake, but she doesn't want to look at them, not when she can feel her skin is still splitting. "I wanted revenge," she says. Her words twist in front of her, ethereal ovals and oblongs that flip over and over.

"On what?" Aion cries.

"On the world, on everything." She shrugs out of desperation; she doesn't know which words to use. "On Kyle. On Riko. And on everyone who didn't believe me."

"Didn't believe you? About what?"

"What Kyle did. I wanted to make everyone pay," she says, and she has. "I wanted everyone to feel how I felt. And this is it . . . This is what death looks like, what it feels like." She lifts her arms, gesturing around them at everyone turned to stone.

"What did he do? Wait. You're *dead?*"

"Slain by the boy who took what he wanted from me and didn't want to face the consequences." She is remarkably calm. "They shoved me out of the tower. Kyle and Riko. The west tower in the castle. It used to have a window—before all of this . . . I don't know why that's gone . . . But Riko and Kyle made it look like suicide."

"Suicide? No, you're not dead." Aion starts to laugh, but then he stops, staring at her body. She doesn't need to see herself to know she is grotesque now, changed beyond recognition.

"I am dead. You read the articles, Aion," she says, and she keeps her voice soft. Everyone read the articles. She remembers that now—because leaving this world hadn't been immediate. She'd hovered in between, before the Gorgons found her. And she'd seen the newspaper reports, learned how her memory had been defamed.

"But you're here . . . And you're her!" Aion points at the Medusa head—the Allie head—in the sky. "And you've been doing this . . . I thought it was Riko?"

"No. It was me. The notebook was mine—the one we planned the summonings in. Kyle took it." And she's looking at him carefully. Because he completed the spell in the west tower room—he must've learned the spell by heart. He finished the summoning for Medusa. "You don't remember, do you?"

Aion's face is blank. He's just shaking his head. "You did *this*? The stonifications . . . my *family*."

She shrugs again. "I needed people to pay. He raped me, Aion. Kyle raped me, and my father didn't believe me. The town didn't."

Aion takes a step back. "Kyle did what?" His face darkens and there's fire in his eyes.

Allie looks down. She can't say the words again.

"Allie, I . . ." He runs his hands though his hair. "Allie, this is . . . I'm so sorry. Why didn't you tell me?"

"I did . . . before. But everyone's forgetting—and it's because of the deal I made. Because the O'Donovans killed me, and I wanted it all to be undone. So I made the deal—and you finished the summoning."

Aion takes several deep breaths. "They killed you?" He swears under his breath. His hands are shaking as he clenches them into fists. "Allie . . . this . . ." He struggles to find the words. "You should've told me," he says. "What they did. I would've believed you. Of course I would've."

"You did—the first time I told you." She tries to smile, but it doesn't work. Her face feels too rigid. "You believed me then—you were the only one who did."

"Then why didn't you just tell me this time?"

Allie lets out a shaky breath. She's now not sure exactly at what point she realized that Aion had forgotten too. Her memories are all jumbled, turned inside out. "It doesn't matter now. What matters is justice has been served." She casts her eyes over the remains of Kyle and Riko.

Then she looks at the other statues. Collateral damage.

"It's all my fault," she whispers. "Everyone . . . all the stonifications. It's because of me." She gulps.

Aion breathes out a long breath, very slowly. "Can you undo it?"

Allie feels cold. So cold. "I don't know."

"You can," a voice whispers, and Allie looks up. There are two more beings in the sky. Euryale and Stheno. Her sisters. She feels a pull to them, and she's in between them, in the sky as well. "You just have to want to. Put it right, Allie, and then you can leave with us."

"Leave?" Allie's heart pounds. At least, she thinks it does. Is she imagining it? Can her heart be beating inside her rotted body if she's been dead for months? She turns to Aion, panic rising in her chest. She can't leave! Where will she go?

"You have to," Euryale says, "else this curse will strike every human."

"But you said I could come back!" Nausea swirls in her.

They said she could come back, and she said she wanted revenge—and she's got it. She smashed Kyle and Riko to pieces. And everyone else who didn't believe her . . . they're statues too. Only it's spread too far, beyond her town, and she can feel it's still growing.

She should go now—shouldn't she? Before she hurts anyone else?

"We did," Stheno says. "But we warned you about Cronus—he's too destructive. He's messed up the timestream, he let that storm loose, and he made people forget the wrong things. He combined his desire for destruction with our powers and that of the Fates, and embodied it all in you—in Medusa's frame. The energy of the world is unstable now, and time cannot hold you here much longer. Come on, Allie. Say goodbye."

THIRTEEN

Tears stream down Allie's face, but her face must have split into raw wounds because the salt of her tears stings, corroding her flesh away.

Aion recoils from her.

"I'm so sorry," she whispers. "I didn't know this would happen." She looks back up at the sky. For a second, she sees Ellie's face in Euryale's and Sarah's in Stheno's. But then her sisters are gone, and she feels their loss as if they've just been snatched from her.

The pain of the loss gets bigger and bigger, and suddenly she's connected to every surviving person in the country who's lost family and friends. Because of her. She tries to disconnect from it, the all-consuming feeling of loss, and she concentrates on the sky, takes over Medusa's viewpoint. But looking down, Allie sees it all. Her vision zooms in one statue, and then another, and another, and another . . . So many, and she's seeing each in close-up snapshots: the frozen tears on a child's face as she took away his life; two elderly women sitting on a park bench; a mother trying to comfort her baby, both frozen. More and more and more images fill Allie's mind, until she screams, breaks the connection.

Shaking, trembling next to Aion, Allie feels sick. She pulls in huge gulping breaths and looks into the sky. "How do I reverse it?"

"You come up here, and you embrace us," Stheno says. "You have to leave that body behind. We didn't think it would get out of hand this badly, but it has. The Fates say you're too strong, you're tangling the life thread, and Cronus knew there would be this much destruction—because that's what he loves, that's what he always gets. That'll be why he said he'd help us. You can't trust men."

Allie's gaze crosses to Aion. No, she *can* trust him. She's always been able to trust him.

"Say goodbye and join us. Join us fully. We will welcome you to our ranks and we need our sister back."

"Medusa?" Allie says.

Euryale nods and points at the beheaded Medusa-Allie in the sky. "You are inhabiting her body, forcing her out. We have to right the order of the world."

"And do it quickly," Stheno says. "It is night-time now and all across the country you're still claiming more victims. And while you can return some of them to life, not all will survive."

Allie nods and gulps. "I'm so sorry, Aion," she says. "I didn't mean for this to happen."

At last, he looks up at her. His face has never looked so angry. She assumes he's furious with her—as he should be—but then he speaks, and she understands.

"If Riko or Kyle somehow wake up from all this, I'll kill them," he says. "They don't deserve life."

Allie nods. "Thank you." She takes a shaky breath as more of her face burns away. "Can you find Ellie? Can you be with her when she wakes up, so she won't be scared?"

Aion nods. There are tears in his eyes.

"Please, go now," Allie whispers.

For a second, she doesn't think Aion's going to leave. That he's going to insist on staying with Allie until she's gone. But then he nods again, the slightest of movements, and turns away.

With a crumbling heart, Allie looks up at the sky, where the ghosts of her new Gorgon sisters float—and more and more of them are appearing, more Gorgons. It's not just Euryale and Stheno behind the Medusa mask. It's a whole sisterhood to welcome her, the transformed souls of countless girls wronged by man.

Allie feels her body lifting up—no, her soul, her essence, because she's looking down too and her rotting carcass collapses onto the rubble.

She knows where to go.

A thousand ethereal lights radiate from her body, and she's still rising, still embracing her destiny, her fate—and with every inch she rises, the lighter she gets, and on earth, one by one, a statue wakes.

She takes one last look back, and her eyes zoom in on Aion's figure as he runs to the west tower of Blackthorne Castle. It seems to take him both forever and no time at all before he is inside, racing up to the tower room where Ellie is. Aion gets there just as Ellie wakes, and if Allie still had a heart, it would be pounding or hitching or catching or something, as she watches life infuse the statue as light floods the room.

Light.

The window—it's back. The tower's returning to normal. The world is returning to normal.

Ellie's fingers move at first, and Aion's shouting in excitement, shouting Ellie's name, reaching out for her. He touches her remaining hand and sees her arm becoming flesh again, then her shoulder, her neck, her face. Allie smiles.

Then she is weightless in the sky, turning, spinning, following the dazzling light that leads to the sisterhood.

"Welcome," the Gorgons say. "We've got you, Maliah. You're one of us now, and we never let our sisters down."

THE END

ABOUT THE AUTHOR

MADELINE DYER (she/her) is a novelist, anthologist, and poet. She is the author of the SIBA-award winning Untamed series and the editor of *Being Ace* (Page Street YA, 2023). She also writes as Elin Annalise and Elin Dyer.

Madeline teaches writing and has a BA (hons) degree in English from the University of Exeter and an MFA in Creative Writing from Kingston University. She is currently pursuing a PhD in Creative Writing at the University of Bristol, where she is researching and writing about traumatized girls and monstrous women in horror and the Gothic.